Eric, Maria, Mom and Dad are travelling back to
their home in the city after a short holiday with
Grandma and Grandpa. Their journey is full of
things to see and places to visit. You can find out
the exact route they take by looking at the small
pictures and working out where they fit in the
large ones.

This edition is
published and distributed
exclusively by
DISCOVERY TOYS
Martinez, CA

First published
in 1988 by
Walker Books, Ltd,
London

Printed in Italy

ISBN 0-939979-20-9

THE JOURNEY
HOME

JOANNE FLINDALL

DISCOVERY TOYS

"Goodbye!" called Grandma.
"Have a good journey home,"
 said Grandpa.

"How long will it take?"
 asked Eric.
"All day," said Mom. "We've
 lots of things planned."

"Let's stop here," said Dad.
"Why don't you two choose
 some cakes?"

Then they were on their way.

"I just saw a little black dog,"
said Maria.

"And there's a little white one,"
said Eric.

"Oh, look, a wedding!"
said Maria.

"And there are the bride and groom," said Mom.

"Slow down, Dad. They're throwing the rice!"

Soon they were out of the town.

"I wish I had a sailing boat like that," said Eric.

"Don't forget about us," said Dad. "We'd like some too."

"That little boy has dropped his strawberries!" said Maria.

"Can we stop and pick some?"
"Sorry," said Mom, "but we don't have time."

"Baaa!" said Maria. "Get out of our way!"

"Hello, great-big enormous white rabbit!"

"Come and see what we've found!" said Eric.

"That foal can't be more than a couple of days old," said Mom.

"I wish we lived on a farm," said Maria.

"Moo!" said Eric. "What are you staring at?"

"That looks like fun!" said
  Eric.
"It's certainly hot enough,"
  said Mom.

"That's the tallest sunflower
  I've ever seen!" said Maria.

"I wouldn't like to be in his
  shoes," Dad said.

"I bet you'd like to be in that
  hammock though," said Maria.

"What luck!" said Dad. "A fair—
and a parking space too."

"I'd like a red balloon."
"I'd like a green one."

"Would you like to have your
face painted?" asked Mom.
"No way!" said Eric.

'Let's buy some sandwiches for later," said Mom.

"I spy something beginning with c," said Mom.

"Hold on to those balloons," Dad said.

"Can we stop and buy some candy?" asked Eric.
"No," said Dad. "We've got plenty to eat."

"It's lucky that dog's on a leash," said Maria.

"Now that's the way to travel!" said Dad.

"That sofa's got pajamas on!" said Eric.

"I'd be afraid to do that,"
said Maria.

"Lots more things with c,"
said Mom.

"I wonder how far they could
go in that," said Dad.
"All the way to China," said Mom.

"They've caught lots of fish," said Eric.

"I'm hungry," said Maria. "Can we eat soon?"

"Good idea," said Dad. "Let's look for a nice place to stop."

"This is a good place for a picnic," said Eric. "Let's stop here."

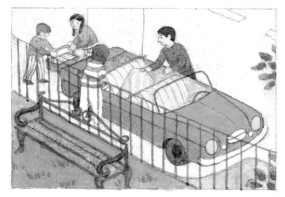

"You two carry the basket," said Dad. "I'll bring the blanket."

"You'll be hungry later if you give it all away," said Mom.

"Look at that boy balancing on the wall," said Maria.

"Hold my hand," said Dad. "We'll cross the street here."

"Toys are upstairs," said Maria. "I saw them in the window."

"This is just like that boat on the pond," said Eric.

"Red or brown?" Dad asked.
"I like the red ones," said Mom.

"I'm glad our balloons are still there," said Maria.

"I can't wait to sail my boat," Eric said.

"That horse is much bigger than the one at the farm," said Maria.

"I've seen that ice cream man outside our school," said Eric.

"I can play better than that," said Eric.
"No you can't," said Maria.

"I wonder who that is," said Mom.

"There are the twins," said Eric.

"And there are Florence and James," said Maria.

"Home at last," said Mom. "It's good to be back."

"This bag is heavy!" said Eric.

"Let's call Grandma and Grandpa
to say we're back," said Dad.

"It's been a lovely journey home,"
said Mom.
And everyone agreed.